Is _____ ns
Bleed When I Floss?

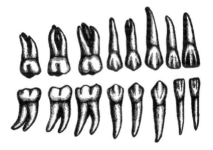

by Blue Sunshine

Curious Corvid Publishing, LLC

Is It Bad If My Gums Bleed When I Floss by Blue Sunshine

© 2024, Blue Sunshine

Published in the United States by Curious Corvid Publishing, LLC, Ohio.

Cover Art by Mitch Green

ISBN: 978-1-959860-29-7

Printed in the United States of America

Curious Corvid Publishing, LLC

PO Box 204

Geneva, OH 44041

www.curiouscorvidpublishing.com

First Edition

Curious Corvid
PUBLISHING

Trigger Warnings

This book contains depictions of SA, mild gore, unhealthy relationships, and grief.

For my siblings,

who are always there for me at my worst,
which is pretty often.

The Permanent Dentition

PART ONE:
THERE ARE SO MANY THINGS

Candy Stains

When we were kids
we put playdough
in our mouths
red, orange, yellow
and bloody skittles
green, blue, violet
fell into our tiny, waiting palms.

We had gushers for tongues,
licking food-safe roaches
squirming and jumping
away from *spit that out.*

When we got old
they went silent
and we filled in the gaps
with monochrome
grout and pebbles and
spite.

Is It Bad If My Gums Bleed When I Floss?

The Tooth Fairy is an Anesthesiologist

The tooth fairy
put me under,
took my two buck teeth
and an extra one
beneath the gums, sprouting up,
blossoming: a bone flower
where it wasn't supposed to be.
I drew it in arts and crafts.

I used to have twenty-one teeth.

The tooth fairy gave me ten dollars
for the pain—
of parting, of stitching me up,
I still don't know.

2004

You didn't keep my baby teeth.
I'm not sure if that's disappointing or
relieving.
I mean, what kind of person keeps a child's
teeth?

Yeah, that's really weird.

…I don't know.
Is it?
I guess I just wanted it to mean more to you
than it did.

Career Day

When I was in middle school,
the smartest girl in my class wanted
to be a dentist.

On career day, she brought floss,
toothpaste,
and a toothbrush
in the pockets of a little white lab coat
her mother had sewn for her.

I forgot it was career day
and I didn't have a mom to sew
white lab coats
so I lied,
took out a pen and a notebook
and told her I was going to be an author.

She played along, asked for my autograph
to show off in the future
so when you get famous, I can say I was your first fan.

She smiled at me—all brackets and wires—
and you know, *god*,
I think she was the first person
I ever loved.

Is It Bad If My Gums Bleed When I Floss?

Nerves

In sophomore year
the smartest, prettiest girl in my class
made bracelets with her friends.
They spelled their names with beads,
pushed holes into seashells,
strung them up on each other's wrists
like their parents gifted
candles and wine.

I asked her to make one for me—
poke holes in the teeth I'd lost
pull them together to make smiles
for my wrists
   to wear happiness on rainbow cords
   to cover scars
   to speak for me
when my lips were tired.

She was lovely. She wrote my name in sharpie
on five teeth—
   flattest, smoothest—
and when she strung them up
on my wrists, I became her friend
and the *clink* was so dull
it was barely heard.

Adolescence

Elegant
that was her
sophisticated her dusty tongue
intricate meanings hidden on
matte bones
strong words beautiful bite
pearly white, no cavities.

Her hydrogen peroxide.

Messy
that was me
clumsy my urgent tongue
silly secrets scribbled on
inflamed gums
all sticky words
filling expanded till it cracked.

My chlorhexidine.

I wanted her incisors
under my pillow.

A Shoulder to Cry On

In junior year,
the smartest, prettiest, kindest girl
in my class
finally got her braces off.
I had never known her
without them.

She came to me first, showed me pictures
before and after
the transformation
from point A to point B
and my eyes caught on an
adorable snaggletooth that,
         with time and heat-activated steel,
eventually fell back in line
with the others.

I silently loved that tooth,
my eye drawn to it
every time she opened her mouth.
I thought, *I love your imperfections*
but she seemed
happier with straight teeth, and
she took such care of her retainer
so I did something for her

13

that I had always struggled with:
I kept my thoughts to
myself.

I still wonder
if she liked me better that way.

Baby Teeth

I wished I were

      —the Milk
she forgot in her
Car.

      —the Nickels
when she said
here's your Change.

      —the Fairy
with her
baby Teeth.

Confession

I always knew I was different
even if saying that sounded
like a mother carefully avoiding
"depressed" and "OCD"
like trying to say
there's nothing wrong with being different
but everything
is wrong with that
because I don't know how to let it *be*.

Mom, you knew that about me too.
Otherwise you would've just said it,
the way I confided *lesbian*
to a friend I
wanted to trust, a friend I loved,
the way I still meant the words
when he interrogated me about my childhood
and pushed me back onto this
little red velvet divan for a Freudian diagnosis.

Mom,
I never felt so unclean
never hated myself more

than when I was so careful
about the placement of
          my teeth
lest he tell everyone I was whore

without knowing
he already had.

PART TWO:
I WANT TO SAY

Natalie

It's Netty, I want to say.
N-e-t-t-y.

I say *here* and then
keep my mouth shut.

The way my birth name
sounds on someone else's lips,
is how *sir* and *ma'am* tastes on my own.

It's almost—wrong. But it's not worth
getting butterflies
in my chest
just to correct him.

> (I bite my lip a bit too hard, a bad
> habit, wince from
> the warm burst of blood
> on my taste buds, the sour tinge of
> iron.
> I lick it off,
> but it keeps
> coming.)

The professor's eyes pass

right over me, and I hate it
more than the way he pressed
my three syllables into two.

Look at me.

He's much older than I am
his hair is graying—he looks like he's scowled
far more than he has smiled
in his entire life.

I worry if he will be strict.

He starts pacing around the room and
stops somewhere near
where I am sitting.
He opens his mouth,
doesn't make eye contact with me.

> (I swallow
> a little bit more
> of my blood.)

What do orthodontists do on a rollercoaster?
Pause.
They brace themselves.

I laugh because it's that stupid and
there are chuckles from
around the room and
he looks so pleased, a real smile
crinkling the corners of his
eyes.

Who the hell wants to hear me talk about teeth?
We have the rest of the semester
for that.

Hahahahahah

He looks at me, finally, as I laugh with
blood on my lips,
and he silently hands me
a tissue.

Look at me.

I like that his teeth
are so perfectly
straight.

Look at me.

I like that his eyes
seem to know
so much.

How to Pretend to be Straighter than You Actually Are

First: ask stupid questions like
Sir, is it bad if my gums bleed when I floss?
because the whole class will look at you like
you're an idiot
but when they start packing up at 2:13,
prepared to leave at 2:15,
your dental professor will call you to the front
of the classroom
and ask you something like
Why did you ask that? or
Do you really not know the answer? or
Are your *gums bleeding?*

Second: say something stupid like
I wanted your attention. or
I just wanted you to look at me. or
Maybe I need to stay after class so you can teach me.
and gnaw at your bottom lip as you glance
away
and wait for him to scold you
for suggesting something so inappropriate.

Third: wait to hear those words that'll
embarrass you
wait, wait
wait

and never hear them.

Anthropophagus

When I first kiss him,
my tongue explores his mouth
curious prodding and flattening
of one muscle against another,
tasting him
  or reading his long life from the texture
  of his molars
    or testing the give of his gums
      for gingivitis
I guess I don't know.

(It doesn't really matter
        when he's the one who pulled me into
        this room
        when he calls me *pretty little thing*,
        when he's over twice my age but I'll
        later let him jerk off
        to my high school photos anyway.)

That afternoon when I run my tongue
over his lip for permission
and he gives it to me with silent parting,
I bite his tongue
pull it between my teeth,

taste copper and something
rotten.

I flinch, so does he, and
my jaw releases him
but we pretend it didn't happen

so we can move on to
the part where
I spread my legs.

I worry, later, in the still of a sleepless night:
if we hadn't broken
would I have eaten him?

Balloon

When I am alone with him,
we share the same air.

I inhale his acidic exhales
let him breathe in my mouth
and inflate my teeth
to oracle balloons.
We tie them on strings
for my peers to pop pop pop
while he explores my gums.

They give easily under his
probing touch
and outside this room
nobody will ever know
          except for you
how easily they do.

Is It Bad If My Gums Bleed When I Floss?

Apostrophe

There was a story in the news the other day
about a dentist who abducted half a dozen
patients
ripped their teeth from gums, one by one
chopped their bodies into   little   pieces
and put their teeth
in a jar
on his fireplace mantel.

It was said that
when they caught him, it was because he
hadn't even tried to hide the jar, a thin layer of
oxidized blood
around the bottom of the glass,
the teeth themselves thoroughly brushed and
removed of
any trace of tissue.
My proudest patients, the dentist—the murderer,
secondly—said. There was no shame and no
fear
of the consequences of his actions.

It was my first time hearing about a killer
dentist.
Until then, it hadn't even crossed my mind

that dentistry may be a field a murderer would
aspire to.
>Maybe he dressed up in
>a little white lab coat on career day
>when he was a child.

It never occurred to me that most dentists
work with children
or what that means for the pedophiles who
want to keep children's teeth,
which implies a lot about who I am
and the person who forced such a realization
upon me.

It's only when his hands wrap around my
throat for the
third time this week,
his fingers worming into my mouth, pressing
my squirming tongue flat
that doubt runs across my mind
dancing with the thought this isn't an
accident—
that everything right here, right now is exactly
as he designed
though he couldn't possibly have known
about
you, a little girl who never saw her father,

or the people who never warned her about
pedophile teachers.

What I did to you was worse. He asked for
your pictures and I
—sent them
without question.
You were already long gone but part of you
never left.

It's when I truly struggle to breathe that
the unraveling sets in *oh my god what have I
done?*
because I realize:
I am an owned thing.
I am the teeth in the jar on his fireplace
mantel.
I am his proudest student.

And there is no undoing
that he has ripped you from my body
or that which he has given in return.

Is It Bad If My Gums Bleed When I Floss?

Milk

Twenty deciduous teeth
and no trace of the scar
where they took a knife to the
       twenty-first.

Milk teeth came and went
just like that
until one day my dentist told me
my permanent ones were
       pretty.

They've grown into the smiling kind,
the type to spill a secret,
lie like it's the
       truth.
And they make a pleasing
silhouette. They like to be admired,
all grown up now, even with wisdoms
not yet erupted,
not like that twenty-first milk tooth.

Now I flash smiles and
laugh like second nature, but I
       bite

when it comes down to
the *no, wait* that is always heard but never felt
quite like the throb
of bone sinking into skin.

> (But I am lying. I lie all the time.
> Except for—the times I don't.
>
> *I'm sorry. I'm late.*
> *No—my period.*
> *Listen to me.*
>
> Ignoring me, one hand caresses my
> face
> the other finds the zipper of
> my pants.
>
> It's supposed to take
> an impossible amount of force
> to bite someone's finger off,
> but I wonder—as he pushes in
> with callouses and roughness—
> if I can at least bite hard enough
>   for my bones to meet his.)

Leprechaun

He works his jaw over my spine
bone on bone
marrow gushes over taste buds
like bad wine
vinegar my blood
oxidize my red—
that's acidic you know
erodes enamel
if he's not careful
it'll stain and
decay
unless he's lucky
and he's a four-leaf clover
his teeth leave scars
dental impressions of the skin
and I—

Is It Bad If My Gums Bleed When I Floss?

Daddy

You ever have a cavity just—
fall out all on its own?
Like it somehow couldn't develop or
more like your gums rejected it.

When I was a kid, my parents gave us
a quarter, a dollar if we were lucky
       except for the once
and I always wanted to give my own
children more than a quarter.
But thinking about it now
curled up, sobbing,
hyper-aware of the skinniness of my wrists
and
the black blood under my fingernails,
I'm so—grateful

to not have children
to lose their teeth
in the first place.

For them not to have a father who encourages
cavity-forming habits
with his own.

I don't want to think about children
putting teeth under their
cotton
          pillowcases

while I give up a dollar for
something I don't even want to
have. So I won't have it. I can make those
decisions now.
I think I get it—what kind of
          person
keeps a child's teeth?

No Tissues

Ever since I met him, my gums have bled.
The fairies fear I forgot how to floss
but I am careful—twice a day it's red,
white cloth scarlet-stained, in the trash it rots.

He won't brush as often as I do, he
still eats food-safe roaches and tongues,
his gums are hard, his teeth are strong, it's
true—
your breath's so bad it permeates my lungs.

I guess humans aren't perfect, but please
brush your damn teeth or don't even kiss me.
I gag on his lips, I gag on my knees
really, it's true, he doesn't deserve me.

Yet, I kneel, swallowing cock so sincere,
so good even *I* wouldn't know I'm queer.

Is It Bad If My Gums Bleed When I Floss?

Size Matters

When I got a cavity filled a few months ago
my first molar on my lower left teeth
the new dentist used a baby needle—
>   red, orange, *yellow*—
to administer the anesthetic.
She got scolded for it:
>   *Netty's big enough to handle the adult needle.*
>   Ironically, spoken as if I were a child.

It was something about having to stick the
patient
more times than was necessary.
I'd like to pretend the needle didn't bother
me,
but honestly, it did.
I had become wary of such penetration.

My dentist, the one who told me my teeth are
pretty,
the one who started the whole needle thing in
the first place,
talked to me while waiting for the anesthetic
to work.

I have a hard time with needles,
but it's not a big deal, I lied
words dragged from my sore mouth.

She looked at me in wonder
as if it weren't normal
as if it were impossible to be afraid of needles,
but—

Why do you have a hard time?

I waited so long to answer
I could feel the anesthetic kicking in
by the time I opened my ~~pretty little~~ mouth
and
slurred out a response.

(Isn't it bad if it hurts when you're inside me?)

My dentist tsked tsked.

My god, what needle is nine inches?
No wonder you hated it.

Netty, do you hear that?

No wonder you hated it.

Sticky

Netty, you've been running
      running
running
your whole life.
Love, isn't it time to slow down?

Isn't it time to put those teeth
back beneath your pillow
to stop letting them do all the talking for you?

Aren't you tired of hiding
all those secrets in the pockets
beneath your gums?

PART THREE:

BEFORE I DIE.

Inadequate

It starts on the edges of my lips
where I was just kissed
creeps in
till it reaches my cheap tongue
and snatches syllables against my teeth.

I give it
two sounds, those Germanic things,
expressing that universal feeling
that I will never be

enough.

That space where tongue meets the back of
teeth
—protoplasmic kisses—
is where it will plunder and ravage and loot
all the secrets I once spoke
all I never let *be*.

I let it crawl along my gums,
pull back the tissue, roots torn wide,
and ease down my throat
—mucus that creeps,

        creeps,

creeps
leaving canals of strep and dysphagia in its
wake—

And just when I start to gag
it'll puncture and probe my soft esophagus
to find a vessel
where it can settle
and rot me from the inside out.

I let it in,
opened my mouth to speak, revealed what
made me weak
when I should've kept my ~~pretty little~~ lips

sealed.

Integration

I asked you once
Do you think we can glue dentures on
to makeshift attraction? Bootleg it. Redneck it.
They didn't have to be pretty teeth, just
normal ones.
To keep the gaps covered
yellow teeth hidden.

You said *those would look better on you.*

I knew that wasn't true
but you had to lie sometimes.
For family.

I said *if the glue doesn't work we can try*
stitching.

Is It Bad If My Gums Bleed When I Floss?

Touch

I brush someone's hand today
passing dollar bills over the counter *here's your*
change
feel the callouses
on their fingertips
minute, rough and tugging
on my skin.

It hits me
so hard I almost puke:
a memory
my oldest enemy
a crawling sensation
of *otherness* I have never properly
described.

It's that millisecond
remembrance of times I touched
Him, Hair
  Lock, Buttons
    Lips.
      It is
        two dozen times.
          Phlegm   Saliva   Blood
            inside.

His rancid breath still
pushes illness into my
        lungs.
The air conditioning still
dries his sweat in my
        pores.
Time still calls for the clandestine brush
of his hand up my inner
        thighs.

Be quiet,
Natalie.

I'd claw my skin off to make it stop
do what I have to. And yet, I let him.

And yet.

I beg to end the thoughts
prickling under skin
but something is   alive   digging into
arteries,
something like oviposition
and a following miscarriage
dissolving my insides like
the acidity in his breath.

My enamel
decayed
so quickly.

I have never been as lucky as him.

Is It Bad If My Gums Bleed When I Floss?

Top 3 Things a Woman Notices about a Man

#1 – His Face.

>He has the kind where, you can tell by
>the wrinkle between his brows,
>he's scowled more than he's smiled his
>whole life.
>I'm not sure why but I want
>to change that.

#2 - His Smile.

(Alt. text: stock photo of a white, blue-eyed man.
He has straight teeth, a strong jaw, and a wide smile.)

>I just think
>they should've picked a different
>picture.
>When I watched *The Good, The Bad,*
>   *and the Ugly*
>all I could think about was

Angel Eyes' *pretty* over
                              bite.
That's what I'd call a good smile. But
this one is dull.
Too white.

Maybe I shouldn't have been a
dentist—
            though I look at this and say
            yes, this is me. I am a woman
            after all,
            maybe also not a woman,
            who notices smiles
            but maybe that is all I am—
because I hate people, and I hate bad
breath,
and I hate going to the dentist.

#3 - His Eyes.

He has the kind where, you can tell by
the dullness in his green irises, he's—

My god, haven't we already covered this?

(Is it too late to say I don't want to do this anymore?)

Is It Bad If My Gums Bleed When I Floss?

Butterbugs

When I was eight
        hanging on to the last of my baby
        teeth,
I captured a butterfly
and a ladybug and
trapped them together in a plastic container,
thinking they would make little
butterbug
hybrids.

The butterfly was the most beautiful one I
had seen
or ever would see:
all white, black stripes, wonky polka dots.
I caught it
    by its wings,
        dropped it into a cage
I'd decorated with
sticks and leaves and drapes made of floss.

I just thought it was pretty.

The butterfly   slammed   itself
against the walls,
until its wings tangled in the floss,

slack material wiggling like a gum flap against
a curious tongue.
The ladybug—an opportunist, a carnivore—
crawled towards it.

The butterfly's wing disappeared first
and its frenzied *flap flap* slowed to a somber
beat…

….. ..

beat…

The ladybug devoured the butterfly
down to its antenna
its twitching falling into sudden
            stillness
like my grandmother after a seizure.

When I got older,
I questioned
why my heart pounded
until the last *flap* of the butterfly's wings,
thrilled with the knowledge I was
watching something die.

I have always been like this.

There are times, still, I fantasize about
stripping a man down by the fiber of his
muscles
until all that remains
is the bloodied mess of bones,
flesh under my fingernails,
hair between my teeth.

> *(Look at me.*
> *Don't you think there is so little of me*
> *left to love?)*

Sometimes, I think about a normal girl
            —a girl I loved too much
            to imagine the copper flush
            of her blood
            on the flat of my tongue.

Sometimes, I think about little
    butterbug hybrids
        that will
            never exist.

Is It Bad If My Gums Bleed When I Floss?

Coffee Stains

It takes a long time
but eventually
I invite you to see me
before time can take your canines
       the shine of your smile
before it softens your roots
until you can no longer speak.

I beckon you over and
you do not come.

I want you to remember me as
someone who gifted you
bracelets and playdough and summertime
polaroids and yellow finger paint
and encouragement.

These shaky hands
cannot caress your face
as they once did,
entreat upon you gentle adoration
never to spurn you, never to hurt you.

This heart
can no longer offer you meaning,

my whole
could not possibly fill your half
you, who have
filled in these gaps of mine
with grout and pebbles and respite.

All by yourself.

I want you to remember me as a person
who was not silent.

And I am ashamed because
I know that you know
       better
than to believe me.

RKO Radio Pictures

This, I reserve, your hand in mine
give you all you deserve
I say sorry again *sorry, sorry*
I want to be enough for you.
If I say *I love you*,
can you say it back?

I met your parents
in a photo album
you keep on the fireplace
mantel.
They look down at me
every time I come over
and their smiles seem to
widen
every day.

I think they're starting
to like me more.

I never told you, but
I didn't mean to hurt you.
It's not an excuse.
I just wanted you to know.

I didn't, didn't—

didn't have parents like yours
who loved their happy little girl
unconditionally
I guess because I wasn't their
happy little girl.

Maybe I gave you up willingly
but I didn't know any better.

I had had—

had so much, but not the
wisdom teeth
to know I should have been worried
if people ever asked me
about the flexibility
of your bones.

People don't have to know
about the things
you've been keeping
beneath the fillings
in your cavities.

That doesn't really help but

I just wanted you to know.

When you leave the room
the glass over your parents' faces
glints at me like Morse code.

Before you get back I
blink—

Blink back a message.

I think it's the most
honest thing
I've ever said
in my whole life.

Is It Bad If My Gums Bleed When I Floss?

Things that Don't Mean Anything at All

The oxidation number of oxygen.
The color of my blood, black.
The puddles I walk through daily despite the
lack of rain.
The gummy kid who waved to me from the
back of a minivan
who probably doesn't know how much it
meant to me
or that he made my entire month.

The autograph an author pulls from the pages
of her own book
      —it's not her name, not her autograph
and
      you know, god, I think it's *mine*—
The way she recognizes me after almost
a decade, because it's been that long since
middle school,
since I gave her that piece of paper with my
name on it.

The way I never once forgot her smile.

The snowfall outside the
window of the cafe she asks to meet at.
A week later,
the house I follow her into
past where ivory-colored flowers
sprout, impossibly, through the snow.

The way she has bone flowers, too.

The stillness of the afternoon when I confide
to her
I have been running away—running running
running
too scared to accept that
I've been longing to take the path
that would lead me straight back
to her.

And none of this matters at all except
she beams at my words
like they mean more to her than
they ever did to me.

Not an Orthodontist

There's a radiation vest
on her chest
>she'd joked, *You're not gonna ask me*
>*if it's possible I might be pregnant?*
and except for her endless quips
she's a good patient,
hasn't complained once.

I might be biased but
I think she looks beautiful
with her mouth
open around a bitewing.

Bite down on this for me, I say.
I'm not thinking about it,
not at first.

She complies so easily
it doesn't mean a thing
but it's *her*, the woman I love,
so all of a sudden it means everything—

Bite. Pregnant. Bite. Soon there'll be blood.
Add enough dental impressions till it becomes
me in that chair and

I let go of the bitewing
stumble away with the force of it
the backs of my thighs hit
a cold desk where a set of
straight teeth *hahahaha* up at me from a glass
jar and
…*Netty?*

Netty. Netty.

Was it something I said?
When I blink,
I see her looking at me with concern,
bitewing in her own hand.
The frown looks wrong on her
because she has spent so much time
doing the opposite.

No, it wasn't.

She reaches for me, and
I let myself feel safe
when I fall into her.
Her lips press chastely
to the scar
on my neck.

I Want Things I Don't Tell People About

For her to cup my face in her hands
like an egg she plans to break, but
not yet—

not yet, not yet, not yet.

To bury myself in her body
until I find the place where
she keeps her soul, stores
the memories of the life she has lived.

To roll her teeth in my hands
throw them down between us and
wish for her good fortune
as a method of flirting:
you're so damn beautiful—

To press my tongue to
the pads of her fingers
and be able to taste
where they have been.

For her hair to be splayed

on my pillows.

For her to be
under my pillows.

To put my hands on her
waist when hers go around my
neck.

To become human again
in her arms
when it's all over.

Use as Directed

Netty,
when you were younger, you only saw
the people out there who were
a lot better than you were.
Kinder, prettier, smarter, richer, skinnier—

You knew, too, there were people who
weren't afraid to say *no,*
and there were people who
didn't lie to the girl they liked
about the things
someone said they did
to the boy from English 101.

But I want you to know:
there are also people
who are exactly like you
and never rinse after brushing
to allow the fluoride to
sit on their teeth,
and there are people who are constantly
dipping
their hands into pure isopropyl alcohol, too.

You can try to explain that to someone
and if your recipient
understands, then she'll know
you mean it when you say
I'm sorry.

Because she loves you, loves you just the way
you want her to,
she'll say *you always liked teeth
more than I did,*
and she'll find the humor in the world
to laugh before
all of that joy spreads
to you.

(Bonus Points) Study Guide for the Upcoming 32-Question Test

Define the following terms using complete sentences.

1. What is "I"?

   I am Netty, a dental student who was once queer, until she decided it was better not to be, and then she made a lot of poor decisions because of it.

   Also study: *my, mine, what words fit within seven seconds of Morse code.*

2. What is "you"?

   You are also Netty, the one who wants to marry a woman and raise butterbugs somewhere in Wyoming, the one who's going to grow up and do exactly that.

   Also study: *pronouns, the ingredients in yellow Skittles, how deep the cervix is.*

3. What is "we"?

   We are you and me—that is to say, Netty and Netty. It's up to debate which Netty is the bigger one and which Netty is simply stuck inside the other.

Also study: *us, our, Einstein's theory of time travel, "Aren't we pretty?"*

4. What is "he"?
   He is Netty's dental professor.
   Also study: *him, his, it, if aging causes tooth decay.*

5. What is "she"?
   She is the love of our life and the person we will grow bone flowers with.
   Also study: *her, hers, the definition of homeostasis.*

The test will be multiple choice.

*Obvious questions (like "is it bad if my gums bleed when I floss?") have obvious answers.

Acknowledgments

This collection would not have been possible without the support of some of my dearest friends and the Curious Corvid community. A huge thank you to:

Christine Danse, author and friend, who read this back when some of these poems didn't even have titles. Her feedback convinced me my poetry was worth sharing, so without her, I would not be writing this now.

Corinne Young, the bextie, who must have collectively spent a full hundred and sixty-eight hours listening to me talk about this since high school. I will always be grateful for the time she has given for the growth of this collection.

The remaining two-thirds of the Tricumvirate, who never cease to feed my creativity and my delusions. I do not know how many of these poems were inspired by unhinged things they have said or done, but I can say for sure that it was A Lot.

Ravven White, wonderful author and publisher, for taking a chance on my work. I have no words to describe how honored I am by the time, effort, and faith they have put into this. It's difficult to believe my poetry collection will stand alongside theirs and the rest of the amazing works in the Curious Corvid community, but I should probably start believing it soon.

Lastly, I would like to thank Mitch Green, artist, for his work on this beautiful cover. When I received the mock-up, I squealed. Very loudly. In public.

Thank you.

About The Author

Blue Sunshine is a poet currently residing near Birmingham, Alabama. Their work explores trauma, queerness, and relationships through the lens of horror, constructing haunting stories around images of the body. They find time to write between classes and shifts at their local coffee shop—but when given the chance, they like to watch Boys' Love, dance alone at the dead of night, or sink their teeth into fanfiction.

Other Poetry Books from Curious Corvid Publishing

I Am Ravven by Ravven White

"*I Am Ravven* is an insightful collection of poetry interweaving themes of love, trauma, grief & growth, and the beauty found in a healing darkness. Ravven's raw and emotional writing style takes you on a journey of self-discovery as she begins to heal from a life of severe childhood abuse. Her honest struggles with mental health, self-image, and feelings of isolation paint a portrait of a victim turned survivor turned warrior. Ravven's poetry is a timeline of highs and lows as she learns how to navigate healing, acceptance, and forgiveness. With an overwhelming message of hope and restoration, *I Am Ravven* shares emotions and experiences that anyone can relate to and empathize with. We all have stories to tell. This one is hers."

Panoramic by Aimee Nicole

"*Panoramic* is a spicy, unapologetic poetry collection examining life after surviving sexual assault and reclaiming sexual identity through

BDSM and inner healing. Kinky, introspective, and real, this collection is one of a kind in the full range of healing and hurt the author explores."

Poems To Read In The Rain by Jennifer Gordon

"A collection of emotionally captivating poetry, *Poems To Read In The Rain* is for those looking for resonance while navigating the complexities of life. Touching on themes of love, loss, grief, mental health, and nature, this collection contains works that can appeal to everyone."

Lady of The House by Grace R. Reynolds

"*Lady of The House* shares the fictional tale of Lady, a 1940s riveter turned housewife trapped by a loveless marriage and societal framework that makes it difficult for her to abandon her current circumstances. She feels purposeless, hopeless, and she is angry. *Resentful.* And she *festers...*"

The Cry of The Ravven by **Ravven White**

"In the beginning, the world was bathed in an eternal darkness filled with terrible monsters and savage deaths. The birth of the first day arrived on the back of a fearless white raven who had dared to steal the sun and drag it closer to the earth. But the sun came with a price and the white raven was burned black by the salvation she so desperately flew for.

Taking the story of the white raven, *The Cry of The Ravven* sheds light on the process of stealing our own suns - working through our traumas in search of a better life. Ravven White writes about her journey from the rawness of a broken heart - healing takes time, healing can hurt, but it doesn't mean it can't be done or that you are alone. Ravven offers you a piece of her sun in hopes that you will find the way to yours. Do you hear her cry? Perhaps it is your own..."

Moonglade by **David E. Grinnell**

"Love, longing, heartache, and loneliness are illuminated in this heartfelt collection from David Edgar Grinnell. Building on themes of budding relationships, misunderstood feelings, and innocent first loves, *Moonglade* creates a narrative that is relatable to everyone looking for love and companionship. Immerse yourself in a world of gothic romantic poetry that shines a soft light on finding and losing love in the twenty-first century."

The Nature of Night by Jenniffer Gordon

"It is the nature of nighttime to be temporary. To be a period of darkness that both begins and ends with the changing of light. And while there are reasons to fear the dark, it can also be a time of deep reflection. A time to study the distance between our arms and the stars. Inevitably, dawn will have its way, and our view of things will shift. This is the nature of night. To show the world a type of beauty that can only be found in darker times."

The Lies We Weave by Grace. R. Reynolds

"Planted ambitions. Wounds that never heal. Cycles of generational trauma that keep us from breaking free of our turmoils. Suffused with Gothic undertones, THE LIES WE WEAVE collection of dark poetry and prose is a journey of self discovery that offers a unique perspective of one woman's path toward healing. Beauty, darkness, pain, and hope can be found along the way so long as we allow ourselves to take those first steps into the unknown."

The Chimera by Michael Perret

"Smarra, a vampire turned from their intersex human form during the Inquisition, is in NewOrleans to feed under cover of an expected yellow fever epidemic. What they don't expect is to fall in love with a Voodoo Queen…

The Chimera is a poetic mash-up of vampires, zombies, incest, slavery, voodoo, and Greek mythology, all while taking its cues from Pushkin's Onegin. The Chimera and Other Dark Poems is a defiantly formal and surprisingly intellectual collection of gothic poetry that explores the patriarchal values that underlie the concept of monstrosity in Western art."

Survived By by Anne Marie Wells

"This beautiful and heartfelt collection is a vulnerable look into an the consuming grief of losing a loved one - and the the love and healing that comes during and after loss. From start to finish, Wells weaves a gut-wrenching narrative that any person who has or is experiencing loss can relate to."

Threadbare by Adanna Moriarty

"Love, loss, grief, and growth are knit together in this uniquely moving collection from Adanna Moriarty. Feel a life flash before you as we follow Adanna on the path of her own – from childhood wonder to young adult freedoms, to budding motherhood and the tragic loss of a parent. Woven with a love only loss could know, each piece brings a nostalgic comfort, causing the reader to ponder the threads of their own life. Moriarty thoughtfully narrates her shift from child to woman and examines the hardest of topics in an honest and gentle way. In doing so, her story is not only relatable but also softens the things we find most difficult to discuss – mental health, adapting to change, and the quiet tragedy of death. This is a collection readers will return to again and again for comfort, for validation, and for the nostalgia of a life well-lived."

Haunted Hallways by **Ravven White**

"What does it take to break a heart? Rejection? Betrayal? Madness? Perhaps a twisted seduction of all three. And what happens when the heart breaks? It rots. *Haunted Hallways* is a complex look at grief and heartbreak through the lens of horror and poetry."

Her Exodus by **Shannon E. Stephan**

"Angels and demons. Heaven and Hell. Faith and doubt. Wolves in sheep's clothing. Cycles of abuse and control that cause us to deny our own intuition. *HER EXODUS*, a collection of dark poetry and prose, takes the reader through the four seasons of one woman's deconstruction journey. As a child, religion taught her to fear damnation and death. As an adolescent, religion taught her to be pure and perfect. As an adult, she recognized the corruption of the church and its leaders, and began asking questions. Follow along as she uncovers her truth. From hiding to healing. From faith to freedom. From needing a savior to saving herself."

Ghost Dance by Aimee Nicole

"In this raw and heartbreaking collection, Aimee Nicole takes us on a journey exploring violence against queer people and the harsh, unforgiving landscape of the justice system. Narrating tragedy from start to finish, *Ghost Dance* represents the story for so many queer victims while calling out for justice, for compassion, and for awareness."